*This book is dedicated to
Leo and Adrien,
who know this song backward and forward.*

Jacket art and interior illustrations copyright © 2014 by LeUyen Pham
Sheet music provided by Musicnotes.com. Copyright © Musicnotes, Inc.

All rights reserved. Published in the United States by Doubleday, an imprint of Random House Children's Books,
a division of Random House LLC, a Penguin Random House Company, New York.

Doubleday and the colophon are registered trademarks of Random House LLC.

Visit us on the Web! randomhouse.com/kids

Educators and librarians, for a variety of teaching tools,
visit us at RHTeachersLibrarians.com

Library of Congress Cataloging-in-Publication Data
Pham, LeUyen.
The twelve days of Christmas / illustrated by LeUyen Pham. —
First edition.
pages cm.
Summary: A newly illustrated version of the traditional song.
ISBN 978-0-385-37413-2 (trade) — ISBN 978-0-375-97205-8 (lib. bdg.) — ISBN 978-0-375-98200-2 (ebook)
1. Folk songs, English—Texts. 2. Christmas music—Texts.
[1. Folk songs—England. 2. Christmas music.] I. Twelve days of Christmas (English folk song). II. Title.
PZ8.3.P537Twe 2014 782.42—dc23 [E] 2013015115

The illustrations for this book were created with watercolor and ink on Arches hot press paper.
Book design by Nicole de las Heras
MANUFACTURED IN CHINA

10 9 8 7 6 5 4 3 2 1

First Edition

The Twelve Days of Christmas

Illustrated by

LeUyen Pham

Doubleday Books for Young Readers

The Twelve Days of Christmas

On the first day of Christmas, my true love gave to me a partridge in a pear tree.

On the second day of Christmas, my true love gave to me
2 turtle doves
and a partridge in a pear tree.

On the third day of Christmas, my true love gave to me
3 French hens
2 turtle doves
and a partridge in a pear tree.

On the fourth day of Christmas, my true love gave to me

4 calling birds

3 French hens

2 turtle doves

and a partridge in a pear tree.

On the fifth day of Christmas,
my true love gave to me
5 gold rings
4 calling birds
3 French hens
2 turtle doves
and a partridge in a pear tree.

On the sixth day of Christmas, my true love gave to me
6 geese a-laying
5 gold rings
4 calling birds
3 French hens
2 turtle doves
and a partridge in a pear tree.

On the seventh day of Christmas, my true love gave to me

7 swans a-swimming

6 geese a-laying

5 gold rings

4 calling birds

3 French hens

2 turtle doves

and a partridge in a pear tree.

On the eighth day of Christmas,
my true love gave to me
8 maids a-milking
7 swans a-swimming
6 geese a-laying
5 gold rings
4 calling birds
3 French hens
2 turtle doves
and a partridge in a pear tree.

On the ninth day of Christmas, my true love gave to me

9 ladies dancing

8 maids a-milking

7 swans a-swimming

6 geese a-laying

5 gold rings

4 calling birds

3 French hens

2 turtle doves

and a partridge in a pear tree.

On the tenth day of Christmas,
my true love gave to me
10 lords a-leaping
9 ladies dancing
8 maids a-milking
7 swans a-swimming
6 geese a-laying
5 gold rings
4 calling birds
3 French hens
2 turtle doves
and a partridge
in a pear tree.

On the eleventh day of Christmas,
my true love gave to me
11 pipers piping
10 lords a-leaping
9 ladies dancing
8 maids a-milking
7 swans a-swimming
6 geese a-laying
5 gold rings
4 calling birds
3 French hens
2 turtle doves
and a partridge in
a pear tree.

On the twelfth day of Christmas,
my true love gave to me
12 drummers drumming
11 pipers piping
10 lords a-leaping
9 ladies dancing
8 maids a-milking
7 swans a-swimming
6 geese a-laying
5 gold rings
4 calling birds
3 French hens
2 turtle doves
and a partridge in
a pear tree.

Can you find all 78 gifts?

The Twelve Days of Christmas

On the first day of Christ-mas my true love gave to me a par-tridge in a pear tree. On the

sec-ond day of Christ-mas my true love gave to me two tur-tle doves and a par-tridge in a pear

tree. On the third day of Christ-mas my true love gave to me three French hens,

two tur-tle doves, and a par-tridge in a pear tree. On the

fourth day of Christ-mas my true love gave to me four call-ing birds, three French hens,

What Are the Twelve Days of Christmas?

The twelve days of Christmas are the days between Christmas on December 25 and Epiphany on January 6. Epiphany is celebrated by Roman Catholics and Protestants as the day the three wise men (or Magi) arrived to visit the baby Jesus. (*Epiphany* comes from the Greek word *epiphania,* meaning "appearance.") Orthodox Christians, however, observe it as the day Jesus was baptized in the Jordan River. It was first declared a holiday in 567 by the Second Council of Tours, a gathering of leaders of the Roman Catholic Church.

Epiphany marks the end of the Christmas season and is celebrated in many ways around the world, with feasts, parties, ceremonies, and dances. In some western European countries, a Twelfth Night cake (or "kings' cake" in France) is baked with a pea and a bean hidden inside. The two people who get the slices with the pea and the bean are crowned king and queen of the evening. In countries such as Greece, Turkey, Jordan, Bulgaria, and Cyprus, Orthodox Christian priests perform the blessing of the waters on January 6 by throwing a cross into a body of water. The first person to retrieve the cross is thought to be blessed with good luck in the coming year.

Traditionally in Europe, the twelve days of Christmas were followed by St. Distaff's Day on January 7, when the household chores would commence after the holidays.

The origin and meaning of the song "The Twelve Days of Christmas" are subject to some debate. It is thought to date from the thirteenth century, but it did not appear in print until 1780, in an English book called *Mirth Without Mischief.* The book presents it as a game in which the leader sings a verse and the next

person repeats it and adds another line, so that each verse becomes more difficult to remember. Such a boisterous game would have been fitting at a joyful Epiphany celebration.

There are several variations of the song, with the gifts in a different order or with different gifts, such as "nine ladies waiting" and "ten fiddlers fiddling." Versions prior to the twentieth century list "four colly birds" (another name for blackbirds, as *colly* means "black as coal"), which later became "four calling birds." "Five gold rings" may have originally been "five goldspinks," another name for goldfinches. With this interpretation, all of the first seven presents would have been birds, which lends credibility to this theory.

In 1979, a Canadian schoolteacher, Hugh D. McKellar, suggested that the song was a catechism that disguised Catholic symbolism when the Catholic faith was outlawed in England, from 1559 to 1829. He suggested, for instance, that the partridge symbolizes Jesus, the two turtle doves refer to the Old and New Testaments, and the three French hens represent the three wise men. There is no written evidence for this claim, however. Moreover, there was no reason for Catholics to hide their belief in these specific symbols, as they were the same for Protestants and Catholics alike.

Ultimately, "The Twelve Days of Christmas" is a celebration of giving. It reminds us of the Magi's gifts of gold, frankincense, and myrrh to the baby Jesus and of God's gift of the Christ child to humanity. As we sing this song at the most celebratory time of the year, we rejoice in the gift of friends and family.